JANE DYER

Little Brown Bear Won't Take a Nap!

 Little, Brown and Company
Boston New York London

For
Brooke and Ayr
with love

First Edition

Library of Congress Cataloging-in-Publication Data

Dyer, Jane.
  Little Brown Bear won't take a nap! / Jane Dyer. — 1st ed.
    p. cm.
  Summary: Unwilling to settle down for his winter sleep, Little Brown Bear heads south
with a flock of geese, but eventually he finds that he misses his nice bed at home.
  ISBN 0-316-19764-5
  [1. Bears — Fiction. 2. Sleep — Fiction. 3. Geese — Fiction.] I. Title.
PZ7.D977 Li 2002
[E] — dc21   2001034447

10 9 8 7 6 5 4 3 2 1

NIL

Printed in Italy

The illustrations for this book were done in Winsor and Newton watercolor
on Waterford 140-lb. hot-press paper.

Dear boys and girls,

This is a book about Little Brown Bear, who lives with Mama and Papa Bear in a cozy little house at the edge of the forest. Little Brown Bear loves springtime, when he and his mama eat birdseed from their neighbor's feeder. He loves the summer, when he and his papa walk in the meadow and gather blueberries. (Little Brown Bear always eats more than he puts in his basket, but Papa doesn't mind!) In the fall, Little Brown Bear's mama climbs up to the top of the highest tree in the orchard and tosses bright red apples down to Little Brown Bear. He loves that! But Little Brown Bear does not like winter, and here is the story that tells you why.

Happy reading,

Jane Dyer

blueberry meadow

bird feeder

train station

Little Brown Bear's house

apple orchard

Little Brown Bear hated to take naps, especially the kind that lasted all winter.

"I won't take a nap!" announced Little Brown Bear.

"Nonsense," said Mama. "Every bear sleeps in the winter. It's time for you to snuggle into bed."

HONK! HONK! HONK!

"What's that?" Little Brown Bear asked his mama.

"Those are geese," she answered.

"Do geese have to sleep all winter?" asked Little Brown Bear.

"No," said Mama Bear. "Geese fly south. But bears sleep, so off to bed you go."

"I want to be a goose and fly south," said Little Brown Bear as Papa Bear tucked him into bed and sang a lullaby. Then Mama Bear read a bedtime story and kissed Little Brown Bear good night.

"Sweet dreams!" they said with a yawn, and they went off to their own bed.

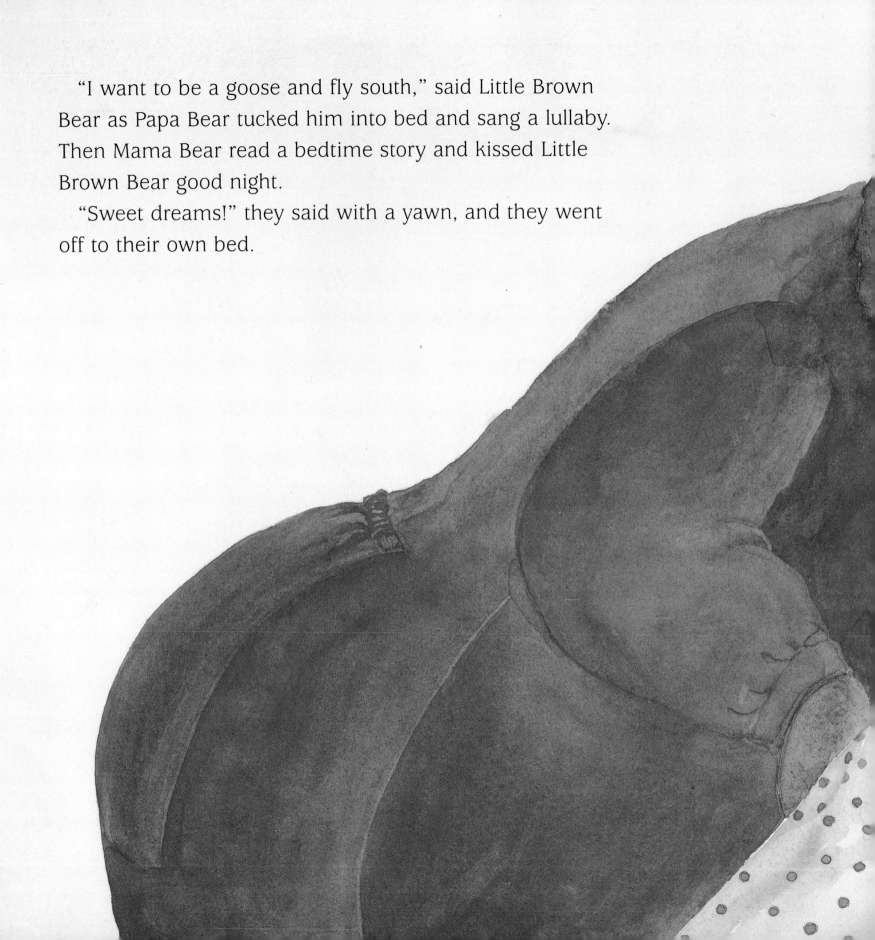

Little Brown Bear waited until he was certain that Mama and Papa Bear were fast asleep. Then he jumped out of bed, packed his valise, and set off to find the geese.

"Hmmm. How will I ever find them?" wondered Little Brown Bear as he headed down the road.

TOOT! TOOT! TOOT!

Little Brown Bear heard a whistle just as a train was pulling into the station.

Gaggles of geese were everywhere. Some geese were boarding the train, some were waving good-bye, and others were leaning out the windows.

"Hop onboard!" called one goose.

So Little Brown Bear did.

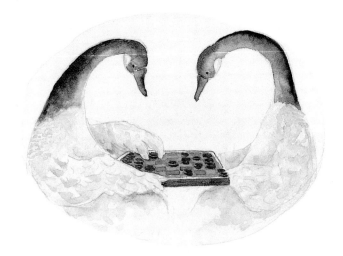

"Why aren't you flying?" Little Brown Bear asked the goose.

"Oh, some of us prefer the train," he answered. "It's more relaxing, and we enjoy the ride."

Little Brown Bear looked around. Two geese were playing chess, others were playing checkers, and another goose invited Little Brown Bear to join in a game of cards. Little Brown Bear thought this was much better than taking a nap!

The next day, Little Brown Bear and his new friends
went to the café car for a box lunch of honey, birdseed,
and peanut butter sandwiches as they watched the
scenery fly by outside their windows. As soon as the train
arrived at their stop, the geese flew off to the beach, and
Little Brown Bear followed.

Little Brown Bear loved the beach. He loved the smell of the sea salt air. He loved jumping over the waves and finding seashells. Most of all, Little Brown Bear loved playing in the sand.

Sometimes he built sand castles with high turrets, and sometimes he made sand pies decorated with seaweed. Then one afternoon, he built a sand cave. It was cozy and warm inside, and Little Brown Bear crawled in to take a rest. First he turned onto one side and then the other. He tried to sleep on his back, and he tried to sleep on his tummy. But he could not get comfortable no matter what he did. Just then a big wave came and washed away the sand cave. Little Brown Bear thought about the nice bed he had at home. He knew Mama and Papa Bear would miss him if he did not return by spring. Little Brown Bear yawned. It was time to go home.

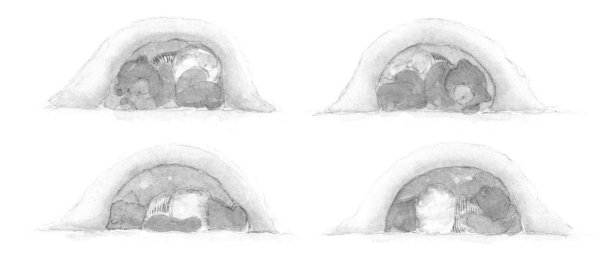

Some of the geese were ready to head back north.

"Please," asked Little Brown Bear, holding back his tears, "may I go with you?"

The geese could see that Little Brown Bear was in a hurry.

"We'll fly you back, it will go faster," they said. The geese fashioned a carrier from a fishing net and safely carried Little Brown Bear home.

Little Brown Bear quietly opened the door, tiptoed past his sleeping parents, and unpacked his belongings. Then he climbed into bed, snuggled under the covers, and fell fast asleep.

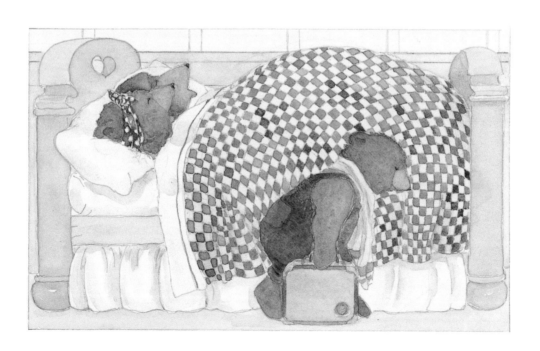

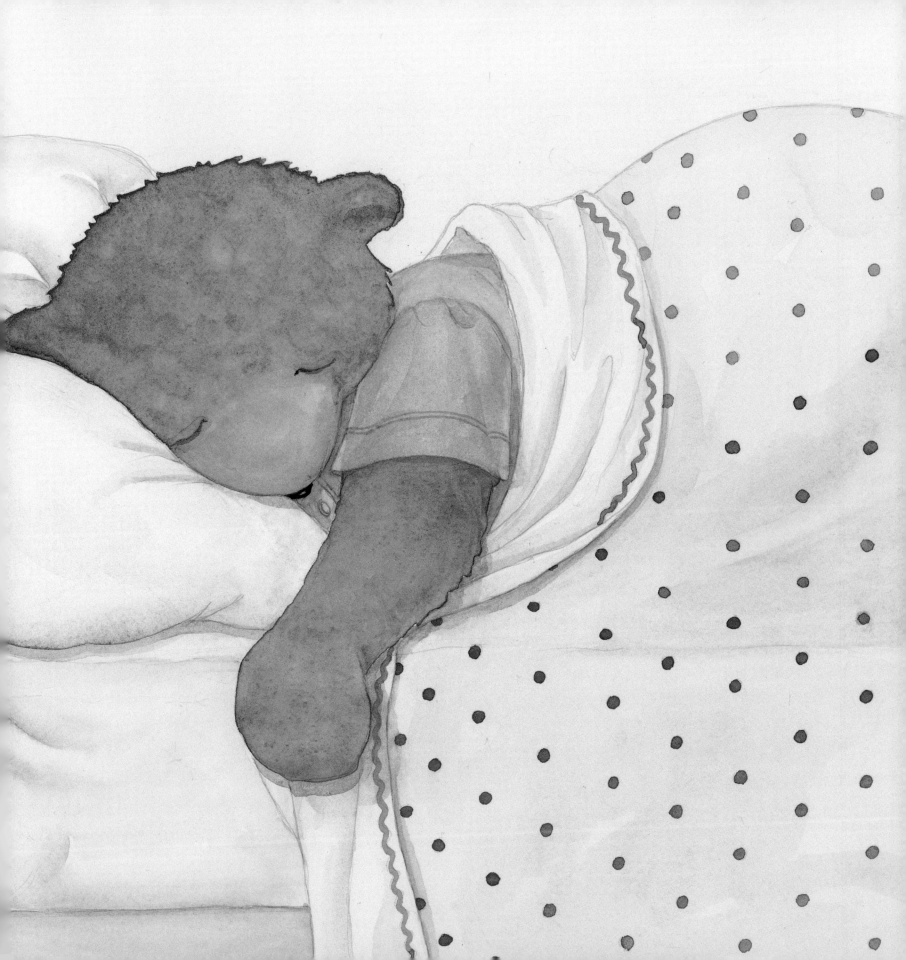

"Wake up!" called Mama and Papa Bear. "You slept all winter," said Papa. "Spring is here!" said Mama.

"I'm not getting up," growled Little Brown Bear. "I didn't even sleep!"

Mama Bear took a warm washcloth and gently wiped the sleep from Little Brown Bear's eyes.

"You silly goose," she said. "Of course you did. You even have sand in your eyes!"

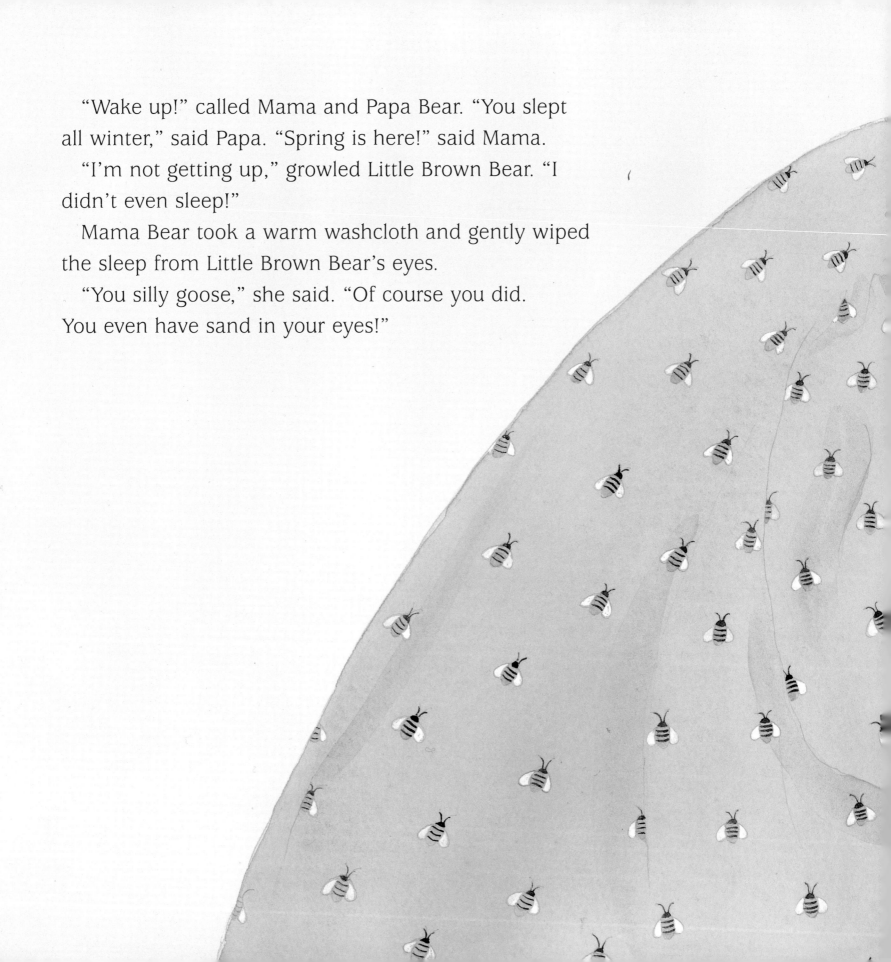

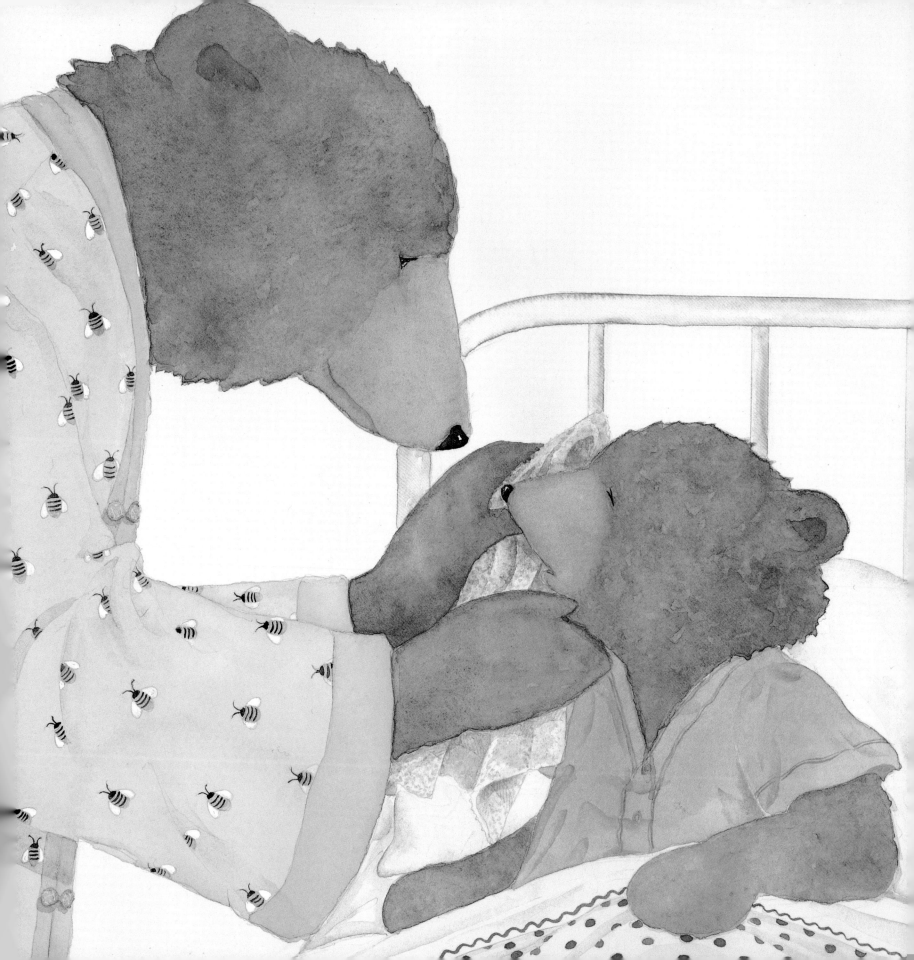